Jenny's Bubble Flight

Michelle Bandel

VANTAGE PRESS
New York

Illustrated by Tanya Stewart

FIRST EDITION

Published by Vantage Press, Inc.
419 Park Ave. South, New York, NY 10016

Manufactured in the United States of America
ISBN: 978-0-533-15951-2

Library of Congress Catalog Card No.: 2007909153

0 9 8 7 6 5 4 3 2 1

To my husband, Bob, my children, Matthew and Andrew (and their future children) and Diana (who already has two of her own, Vanessa and Nicholas)

Contents

Jenny's Bubble Flight

One
Jenny's Bubble

Jennifer found her bubble bottle on the wood floor. She had been standing on the back porch of her small house, gazing at the sparkling ocean. She turned the aluminum bottle cover slowly until it came off. With her pointer finger she felt around gingerly in the soap solution for the plastic stick with the ring at the bottom. She pulled it out carefully and began to lightly blow through the tiny ring. As she puffed softly, the prettiest rainbow-colored bubbles were released from the brittle ring. Many flew out, scattering over the backyard fence and toward the rich blue ocean.

Jenny liked to blow one flawless bubble at a time. She watched one as it gradually changed from green to yellow to pink and then to clear. It formed a shimmering sphere and then floated easily away from her. She did not even dunk the pink ring back into the soap solution until the previous bubble was either drifting too far from her to see or until it glistened and then popped.

While she blew the bubbles precisely one after another, she pondered her mother's health. Mrs.

Waverly had been unusually sick for two months now. No one was able to explain to Jennifer what was happening. Her mother had always been the type of person who enjoyed just being with her family no matter what they were doing. In the past few months this had abruptly changed. Each time Jenny had proposed a family outing to her parents the suggestion was met with refusals. Her father kept expressing regret that it was not a good time for traveling. Jenny understood her mother was ill, but still blamed her mom for making her stay home day after day during the summer vacation from school.

Jenny watched curiously as a stunning monarch butterfly lilted from branch to branch on her mother's pink camellia bush nearby. It flew suddenly onto the covered porch and then landed gracefully on the eight-year-old girl's petite shoulder. Jenny held still for a moment to study it and then continued playing.

Blowing this last bubble had become a lengthy chore for some reason. No matter how much air she blew through the wet ring, the delicate bubble would not release itself. It began to grow larger and larger until Jennifer felt the slippery, clear soap solution surrounding her. She could breathe easily and she could see perfectly the churning ocean in front of her and the homey beach house behind her. The transparent soap film enclosed Jenny from the top of her brown-haired head, around her red blouse and blue jeans, down under her white running shoes.

Jenny sensed movement and a lifting motion sort of like the giddy sensation that she had when she was riding up in a hotel elevator. Pushing on the bubble wall from the inside was easy. She did not burst it though. The glittering sphere, with Jenny inside, began to rise freely above the garden fence. She had risen so high that she would not dare step out even if she could.

Suspended this way, inside this clear ball, was very scary and soothing at the same time. Jenny did not even care how it was happening or who was making it happen. She just wondered where this peculiar bubble was taking her.

A fluttering movement tickled her tensed shoulder. The black and orange butterfly was still sitting on her cotton blouse, but nervously flapping its colorful wings. Jennifer faintly heard a tiny voice say, "What is happening? I've never flown this high before."

Glancing all around her, Jenny could see no one in the bubble with her.

The little voice spoke again, "Where are we going? I only wanted to watch you play with bubbles."

Jennifer was surprised when she instantly realized that the dainty sound came from the exquisite butterfly. It took a moment for her to answer, "I don't know where we are going. But, look how far we can see! We are above the ocean and I can see people walking and playing on the beach. Look at the seagulls and driftwood floating in the water!"

Jenny considered why the children who seemed to be looking up toward her did not show any amazement. Couldn't they see this gigantic bubble containing a troubled, brown-haired girl? She asked the friendly butterfly, "Why don't those people help us get down? Don't they know we're up here? They're staring into the sky but they don't seem to see us. How can this be?"

The enormous bubble had been wafting in the air over the sun-drenched ocean with absolutely no sign that it was being watched. Jenny concluded, "We must be invisible!" and she was glad.

"I think you're right," stated the kind butterfly. "I suppose since we are sharing this bubble, I should tell you my name. I am called Tiger because of my coloring."

"I'm glad you're here with me," said Jennifer. "What a surprise to be flown away in a bubble on the same day that I meet a talking butterfly! My father sent me outside to play so he could spend some time with my mother. I thought I would be bored, but I'm sure not."

"Why did your father tell you to play outside?" asked Tiger.

Jenny explained to the amiable butterfly that her mother was really sick. "My father looked very worried. He is always frowning when he is home. No one wants to play with me and I always feel I'm in the way. I'm too young to help."

"Are you worried now too?" the butterfly inquired.

"Yes, I am," said Jenny. "I shouldn't be here in this bubble. I should be helping my mother. I don't know why she is ill now. The doctor doesn't know what's wrong. I'm not much use to her sometimes because I get so bored staying close to the house."

Tiger flew to Jenny's right hand, settled softly on her index finger and said, "Maybe I can help too."

Jenny could hear no noise except the slight sound of air passing around the comfortable bubble. The mild breeze began to take her even further away from the sandy land. At the same time, she could feel herself floating higher and higher. She could barely make out the clustered houses in Seaview anymore. She certainly could not have seen the expressions on people's faces even if they were aware of her inside the clear sphere.

"Look, Tiger, our bubble has glided above the clouds! I can't even see the beach or the cliffs where my house is."

The sympathetic butterfly responded, "I'm afraid it may be awhile before you see your home again."

Jenny had become tired of standing and was now able to sit down inside the soap solution without puncturing the flimsy walls. She was grateful for this because a break in the huge bubble would have been a certain catastrophe. The translucent bubble was high up in the sky at this time.

"I feel like an angel or an eagle gliding in the sky. It's so quiet up here."

The considerate butterfly remained silent so Jennifer could enjoy what seemed to be a magic spell.

At times the wandering bubble would carry Jennifer past small flocks of hectic birds. Somehow she knew that even these swarming birds did not see her. She was not concerned that they might burst her silvery globe. A feeling of calm and trustfulness soon lulled Jenny to sleep.

Two
Hummingbird Guides

A slight quiver of the hovering bubble awoke Jenny suddenly. As she rubbed her sleepy eyes she was startled to see a small flock of gorgeous lime-green hummingbirds surrounding her shimmering orb. Each charming hummingbird was dressed mostly in these bright green feathers. Each one had a spotless white throat and a bright magenta-colored chest. With their slender, long beaks pointed straight in front of them, they seemed to be guiding Jenny's sphere.

The bobbing bubble was moving more swiftly now than it had been on its own. The furious fanning of the hummingbirds' wings were forcing them to speed through the puffy clouds and then out into the most beautiful baby blue sky.

"Tiger, it feels as if we're being guided like a stick on a river current. We must just go where we are led."

Jenny was able to take her inquisitive eyes off the occupied birds for a few moments. She spoke excitedly to Tiger who was wide awake now too, "Do you see all those pretty islands in the middle of the green water? They seem to be deserted."

Tiger replied, "Yes, they do, but these eager hummingbirds are directing us down toward them. Maybe there is someone there who wishes to see you."

Aiming Jenny's transparent bubble toward the smallest of the islands, the experienced humming-birds were slowing the frantic movements of their glossy wings slightly. Before Jennifer could have counted to ten, she was standing on this skimpy piece of land. It was not any larger than the shopping mall in her hometown.

Tiger was still resting on her fanned hand. Deeply breathing the fresh air, Jenny announced, "It smells just a bit like coconuts."

Tiger fluttered hastily to a sizeable patch of pale yellow flowers and observed, "These flower petals are so soft."

At this instant Jenny was aware that her protective bubble was gone. Somehow in this past moment it had disappeared. "Our bubble is gone, Tiger! How will we be able to leave this island when we're ready?"

She had barely begun to really look around her when out from some of the flower shrubs came a slightly strange-looking bird. Jenny knew it was alive because it was moving. She wondered why she had never seen such an exotic animal in any zoo or any book before. The slim head of the peculiar bird resembled a dove. It was glowing white with two blue beady eyes situated on either side of it.

The shape and size of the unusual body were similar to that of a stately peacock. The abundant feathers on the bird's body were not turquoise and green, though, like the common peacocks that Jenny had seen in pictures. The chest feathers were a dark purple which gradually lightened to a lilac color near the elongated tail. The long flowing tail feathers on its train were black and white. When the bird fanned its extraordinary tail one could imagine dozens of spooky eyes staring out.

Jenny gasped with pleasure and said, "It's so amazing, Tiger. Can you see it from where you are?"

The magnificent bird paraded proudly toward Jennifer. She could tell immediately that this was the most respected creature on the island. The other more ordinary birds which had gathered stepped respectfully to one side. The distinguished peacock was given plenty of space to enter the hushed clearing in which Jenny was standing.

Then the most startling thing happened—the elegant peacock spoke to Jennifer. Its tan beak did not open even the slightest bit, but from its impressive body came these tender words, "I welcome you to our little island. As you can see, we birds make this our permanent home. We travel all over the world throughout the year. You humans seem to

think that we fly to certain places to escape bad weather. In truth, this island is our home and we only visit your crowded cities in order to learn about your kind."

Jennifer was stunned for a minute. Because everything was quiet, she realized that the kind peacock was waiting patiently for her to speak. She felt that she should curtsy before addressing this regal animal.

"I am sorry to have disturbed all of you. This morning I found myself caught inside a bubble with my new butterfly friend. We floated through the sky without being able to steer the bubble which was carrying us. I don't know why we were brought to your peaceful island, and I don't know what has happened to my orb. If you will help me find it, I will once again leave you to yourselves."

After spreading its tail feathers even wider, the accommodating peacock stated, "There is no need to go so soon. I commanded the hummingbirds to guide your globe to our island. We need your help if you will be so kind. You are welcome to remain here as long as you wish. We enjoy the company of humans and can learn much from you."

All of the time that the intelligent bird was speaking, its sharp beak still did not move. Jenny was very curious about how this was done. She did not think it would be polite to probe. Instead, she asked the gracious peacock, "How can I possibly help you? I am only a child."

Three
The Peacock's Request

The splendid peacock answered, "Children are wonderful! Sometimes they can help when no one else is able. I have a reason for bringing you to our tiny island."

The clever bird settled down into the soft grass that covered the serene clearing. It explained, "We birds are able to fly all over the earth and still live on this island together. Many of us travel hundreds of miles each day to gather information about you humans. In fact, most of our members are gone now. Our vital wings would very likely be continuously sore and incapable of carrying us to all of these wondrous places. We have the good fortune though to know where there is a useful fountain of special nourishment for us.

"There is such a valuable spring filled with the most beautiful emerald-colored fluid in a hidden cave hundreds of miles from here," it continued. "Each year one and only one brave, strong bird is chosen to make the extensive journey for the rest of us. That solitary bird must carry our priceless vase in its sturdy beak. It must fill it at this precise fountain and return it to us. The irreplaceable vase has a cover so that on the trip back to the island none of its precious contents is spilled."

The resolute peacock completed its statement, "This year we chose the golden eagle to use his powerful wings to travel to the distant spring. The proud eagle accomplished his honored task. Unfortunately, while gliding over our island to land, he accidentally dropped the heavy vase into a small pool. Because we are birds, none of us is able to retrieve the urn. All of this essential liquid which was brought last year is gone. We cannot wait another month for a second envoy to collect it. We are desperate and we are begging your aid."

"I still do not understand how I can help you," Jennifer stated. She was very puzzled, but quite willing to assist the needy birds if it was possible. All of this talk about a secret cave with a mystical spring of special nourishment made her consider a solution to a problem. Some of this marvelous fluid might be just the thing to cure her ailing mother.

The royal peacock at this point noticed the unhappy confusion on Jenny's face. It decided that before relating the birds' request to her, everyone might do a lot better after eating some overdue lunch. With a gentle flap of its broad wings, this magnificent bird entreated some of the lingering blue jays and cardinals to bring Jennifer her favorite food.

Jennifer walked leisurely to the yellow flowers where Tiger had been resting while the solemn peacock talked. She held out her index finger for the eager butterfly to grasp. As she took Tiger to the tranquil clearing she could see plates heaped with tacos and chewy chocolate brownies set out on a picnic cloth before her. Astonished, she asked, "Tiger, how did they know what I love for lunch? It looks delicious."

Jennifer hungrily ate three spicy tacos and shared brownie crumbs with the polite butterfly. The concerned peacock patiently watched Jennifer drink the last swallow of her sweet pink lemonade.

After the young girl had patted her mouth with a cloth napkin and had placed it on her lap, the bird said, "Now I must really ask you to listen well to my request. We know that some humans are able to swim very well and some can even dive to great depths. The clear pool in which the rare vase is resting is about twelve feet deep. We are able to see our priceless urn sitting on the bottom. Thankfully it did not break in the fall.

"I have to ask you," it questioned. "Are you able to swim and can you dive that deep? Would you be willing to attempt to fish out this most precious container for us? There are some jagged rocks near the sides of the pond and some cover patches on the bottom. We are confident that since you are still a small human, you are more capable of doing this than others might be. Your petite size is a blessing. You can dive into the center of the pool without scraping your skin or bumping your head on some of the rocks."

Without having seen the pool, Jenny could not imagine that this simple request could be very difficult. She asked Tiger, "Do you think I can do this?"

The prudent butterfly remarked, "I think you should try, but maybe you should study the pond first before you decide."

Overhearing the tiny butterfly's comments, the thoughtful peacock said, "I think your friend is wise. Please follow us to the pool. We will show you what you must do before you make up your mind."

Four
The Angry Pond

Since the complete island of the birds was not large, the festive parade of the many species of birds led Jennifer to the nearby pond within about ten minutes. This was the first chance that Jenny had to really get a good look at the many types of birds that lived on the undisturbed island. Some of the kinds she had seen in her backyard at home and others she had seen at the zoo, in the forest, or at the beach.

The grand procession consisted of red-breasted robins, the pleasing blue jays and brilliant cardinals that had served her yummy lunch, some gorgeous orange and black orioles, tiny brown sparrows by the hundreds, and dark black larks. There were even some curious owls that had remained awake because of all the excitement.

Two golden eagles glided watchfully overhead. Jenny whispered secretively to Tiger who was riding on her shoulder, "Which of those eagles do you think dropped the birds' vase into the pond?"

The pensive butterfly did not have time to answer since Jennifer had to stop quickly to let some toddling quail march across the path. Their crests were bouncing absurdly and a number of chicks followed closely.

Three laughing gulls flew between the towering trees. They seemed to wear their black masks as disguises to hide their identities and the reason for their snickering. An enormous vary-colored toucan directed the busy proceedings as Jenny entered a small treeless clearing. Some beautiful black-billed cuckoos were calling the clamorous parade to order. Lastly, a lone woodpecker was attempting to quiet the crowd by tapping on an imposing tree. The anxious peacock wanted to explain to Jennifer what needed to be done.

Calling Jenny to the side of the swirling pond, it said, "Come here, close to me, but watch where you step."

It adamantly motioned to her to look into the water in order to see where the crystal vase had fallen. As she bent hesitatingly over the edge Jennifer was surprised to observe that the dive would be difficult. There were indeed many jagged rocks surrounding the pool. They also lined the sides and bottom inside the pond.

Jenny caught a glimpse of the emerald-colored vase at the bottom. When she leaned over she had the sensation that the water began to roll and splash. Now it was not just a quiet pond. It was a small ocean with white waves breaking against the sides. This really seemed ridiculous since the entire pool was only the size of her bathroom at home.

She peered in surprise at the watchful peacock and asked, "Why does the water act this way?"

It replied, "We do not understand the behavior of this pond. We used to drink safely here. Since the vase was dropped into the pool six days ago though, we have noticed some obvious changes in it. What used to be a small, peaceful pool containing delicious, clear water is now a surprisingly greedy body of water. Anytime anything leans over it, the pond grows very irritated and jealous. I think it means to keep our precious vase forever."

After listening attentively to the peacock's explanation, Jennifer attempted to study the active pond again. She wanted to decide if she really might be able to make the dangerous dive to the bottom. She bent again over the foamy water. She was splashed once more and thoughts of a fall off a cliff when she was younger flashed into her mind. She sat down suddenly because she felt dizzy. The numerous birds began to chatter restlessly among themselves and the caring peacock gracefully walked to her side.

"What is wrong, Jenny? Tell me. I can help you."

Jennifer swallowed hard and haltingly explained to the bird, "Two summers ago my parents and I were strolling along the beach one evening. It is only a block from our house in Seaview. Our home and the neighbors' homes are all built on a cliff that faces the ocean. At some points along this cliff there is no beach covered with sand. There are only boulders that seem to have been rolled up to the cliff by some careless giants. The half-buried boulders are continually being doused with waves which slam up against them and cover them with cold saltwater."

She continued, "We were walking in the sand when I asked if I could climb a sloped part of the cliff. I wanted to look down on my parents from above. I ran ahead and scrambled up the cliff within a few moments. When I reached the top I decided to get a better view of the beach. I walked along the edge until I was overlooking some boulders below. My father shouted to me from the sand. I raised my hand to wave to him. My foot slipped! When I slid over the side of the cliff I grabbed the tangled root of a tall tree which was sticking out from the loose dirt."

"My parents saw me fall, but they were about a block away from me and below me too. My father raced up the same side of the cliff that I had climbed. While he was running he kept shouting to me that everything would be okay. It probably only took one or two minutes for my father to grab my wrists. He finally touched me when I was really beginning to feel weak and queasy from staring below at the pounding waves. I'll never forget how scared I was—all those boulders and crashing water."

As Jennifer finished her brief story she trembled with the same fear she had felt on that perilous cliff.

The steady confidence that she had felt at lunch had disappeared.

Tiger fluttered hastily to her flushed cheek as if kissing her and then landed on her tense finger. The vigilant peacock folded its wings around her until she became calm again. Her self-assurance gradually was pressed back into her with the warmth of its comforting wings. Jenny looked at the understanding peacock with complete trust. She knew within her that this magnificent, caring bird would not let anything harm her.

The reliable peacock did not need to say anything. It fanned its tail feathers and turned around so that all the assembled birds could see its determined face. They knew it was time to quiet down once more.

Slowly, the peacock said, "I will be right here beside you when you dive. I know that the task is difficult. Remember that I chose you for your size and swimming skill. You can do it! Our future is at stake and we are depending on you."

These encouraging words were all that Jennifer needed to hear. The ruffled chatterings of the other birds were muffled. She made up her mind once more to perform this urgent feat for the needy birds. She also knew certainly that if she remained frightened of this buffeting water, she might never be able to feel proud of herself again.

Jenny spoke briefly to Tiger, "You need to leave me so I can dive into the water. I know I can get that vase."

Tiger flew soundlessly to a large grey rock. Jennifer watched him and then took off one shoe without untying it. She placed it deliberately on the grass and then slipped off the other one and put it beside the first. Next she removed the bright red socks she had pulled on her feet that morning. Jenny thought what a long day this had been already and it was only a little after noon.

Jennifer did not have a swimsuit with her. She would have to undress before hundreds of birds she didn't really know well, yet. Being shy, Jenny decided to dive dressed in her jeans and blouse. She would worry about drying her clothes later.

Jenny was a good swimmer. She could hold her breath for two minutes while swimming in her neighbor's pool at home. Swimming in a calm backyard pool though, might be a lot different than swimming in this fuming pond. The water here rose in waves at times. She gave the royal peacock one last look that meant, "I'll try, but be there for me if I fail."

Pushing her hands high above her head, Jenny took a long, deep breath. She leaped forward over the spiked rocks which lined the side of the pond. She courageously dove straight into the center of the pool. The waves splashed around her disappearing legs. Opening her searching eyes, Jenny could see

the unbroken vase and the rough rocks lying around it. The water was churning and tugging her away from her goal. She kept pulling the water out of her way with her cupped hands and reached the guarded vase with this first breath.

Just as she touched the slippery vase, she felt the pressing need to swim to the top of the pool for air immediately. The shielded urn was lodged tightly between two heavy rocks. It was impossible for Jennifer to take the time now to try to loosen it. She looked to the top of the deep pond and swam upward as fast as she could.

When her head popped out of the water she opened her green eyes. All of the fretful birds were observing her. They knew she had failed and she could see disappointment on their faces. But they did not know Jennifer.

She took an enormous breath of air and plunged back into the cold pool. She swam furiously to the stony bottom. This time she did not allow the moving water to yank her away from her goal. She reached the vase in only fifteen seconds and used her slender fingers to pry the rocks away from the precious treasure.

Securely holding the breakable vase with both of her hands, she forced her lanky legs to move. Determinedly kicking her feet, she drove herself to the surface of the pool once more. As soon as her face felt air, she again sensed a rising movement that she had experienced in her soap bubble.

The golden eagle that had dropped the vase into the pond had grabbed Jenny's dripping shoulders with his mighty talons. She emerged elatedly from the waves and he carried her away from the jagged edge. The strong bird gently placed her on the plush grass near the noble peacock. The angry pool threw one last huge splash of water on her.

Jennifer could hear the enthusiastic cheering of the ecstatic birds while she was catching her breath. The grand peacock itself brought her a warm cloak of bright yellow feathers. It wrapped it cozily around her. Jenny did not shiver and within a moment did not even feel wet. It was as if all the water had been absorbed into the luxurious robe.

When she easily lifted the fluffy feathers off her shoulders, Jennifer shouted, "Look, I'm completely dry. I'm going to put on my socks and shoes."

Tiger flew circles around her saying, "You're a heroine, Jenny! You should be so pleased with yourself."

Jenny smiled from ear to ear and triumphantly admitted, "I am."

She at once held out the costly vase to the dignified peacock. It bowed to her and then victoriously displayed the desired urn for all the birds to view.

Five
A Well-Earned Rest

Jenny had never seen such a chirpy, excited group of birds in her life. The joyful peacock flapped its sturdy wings. Before she knew it, she was sitting on a soft, orange silk cloth that was stretched tautly between the agile beaks of four large seagulls. They waited meekly as Tiger flew back to Jenny's shoulder.

"You're terrific!" he congratulated her.

These humble gulls then eagerly carried her back to the same clearing where she had originally landed on the island. They floated above the heads of all the other birds that were parading back on their funny feet. Jenny really did feel almost royal herself as the thankful peacock greeted her with another deep bow.

"We are very grateful to you," it said, "for the accomplishment of our risky task. The sun is beginning to set. We beg you to let us prepare a feast in your honor. Please stay the night with us on our island and accept our hospitality. I know you are concerned about your mother and how you will be able to leave the island. Tonight we will give your problems some thought. Hopefully we can propose some effective solutions in the morning. Until the sun rises with a new day, please enjoy yourself. Let us show you our immense thanks for returning our precious vase and its contents."

"Thank you. My little friend and I will be glad to stay overnight," Jennifer told the generous peacock as she curtsied.

The superior peacock turned gracefully, being careful not to brush its fanned feathers against the surrounding thick bushes. It slowly left the crowded clearing followed by many types of owls. They would undoubtedly decide together how they would help Jennifer regain her elusive bubble. She would have to wait to see if they could also help her discover a cure for her sick mother.

Jenny had not noticed before, but while she contemplated the peacock's stately exit, energetic birds had been spreading an evening banquet for her on the velvety grass. Her tired eyes sparkled as she saw the astounding amounts of appetizing food laid out before her.

Tasty pepperoni pizzas, candy-covered doughnuts, ice cream sundaes, barbecued hamburgers covered with all the condiments she could have imagined, more tacos, plump juicy hot dogs, chocolate chip cookies, various frosted cupcakes, crunchy potato chips and buttered popcorn filled the numerous plates on the spongy grass.

"Tiger, I'm going to try everything. It all looks so delicious!" Jennifer said happily to the faithful butterfly.

Tiger had already hastened from her secure shoulder to nibble his favorite things. The courteous birds waited for Jenny to finish. Once she was done, they too enjoyed the plentiful feast. Amazingly Jennifer did not become ill from eating too much junk food. She vaguely guessed that this was due to the peacock's magic.

After such an adventurous and surprising afternoon Jennifer confessed to the attending birds that she was sleepy.

"I would like to take a nap," she told them.

Four agreeable lovebirds immediately prepared a large down-lined nest. It had been made into the spreading branches of a strong old oak tree.

Jenny offered, "I can climb the tree myself."

The golden eagle shook his curved head and lifted her effortlessly once again. He gently placed her limp body in the woven nest. Four miniature sparrows covered her carefully with a pastel pink quilt to keep out the chilly night. The velvety quilt was warm, but only felt like air when it was pressed over her tired legs. It was so delicate and soft.

Jennifer found a turquoise silk pillow that was the perfect size already laid in the soothing nest. She snuggled deep into the down of the roomy nest, wiggling with pleasure. The only sight before her eyes was the remote top of the tree with its green leaves rustling in the murmuring breeze. Black sky peeked through the canopy of leafy limbs.

Tiger was settled on the puffy quilt near Jenny's motionless hand. At home Jennifer would have rejected the suggestion of going to bed for the night at six o'clock in the evening. Tonight she welcomed sleep keenly.

Jennifer blew Tiger a brisk kiss.

"Good night, brave friend," he said.

Having complete trust in the clever peacock, Jenny gladly gave in to her dreams. Bubbles floated before her closed eyes. There were bubbles in the water and bubbles in the air, all glistening and sparkling. They grew bigger and bigger and then popped, spraying Jenny with tiny droplets of water. At first, the spheres were clear, but then Jennifer could see familiar images in them. Her loving mother smiled at her from one, her protective father grinned in one, and the peacock's handsome face floated in the last one she recognized before drifting off to a desired sleep.

Six
Solutions Found

Jennifer awoke lazily to the musical sound of cheerful songs of hundreds of birds chirping together. They were compactly perched in the strong boughs of the trees that encircled the immense oak in which she had slept. She sat up drowsily in the cozy nest and stretched her arms above her head. Tiger had already fluttered away. Climbing out of the spacious nest was not difficult for her. She promptly spied the regal peacock resting on the luxurious grass at the bottom of the tree trunk. It seemed to have been waiting for her.

Speaking clearly, the official peacock said, "I hope you have had a restful sleep in my favorite tree. The logical owls have spent much of the night with me speaking of your problems. We have decided among us that we must tell you the directions to the cave in which our precious nourishment is found."

"We have never revealed this to any other group of animals. It has forever been a guarded secret of which only birds are aware. We have the willing agreement of all the birds on this island. They feel that you deserve this information from us. Without your help we may never have been able to send an envoy there again."

The majestic bird continued, "As to the immediate problem of finding another bubble in which you can travel, we are confused. The knowledge for making another such orb is not within us. We have discussed this problem with each other."

"Our decision is to allow you to search through our treasure nest. We hope that you will find something you can use to leave our island. We wish to remind you that you are welcome to remain with us for as long as you like."

The reassuring peacock concluded, "The eccentric pigeons seem to bring back the most treasures from their interesting flights. Some of them will lead you to our riches."

Jennifer smiled and confidently said, "Thank you, your majesty. I should be able to find something to use."

She looked about her for Tiger. Not seeing him, Jenny shrugged and thoughtfully followed the peculiar pigeons through the thick bushes and along the dirt pathways. These worn trails seemed to have been walked many times. Of course the squat pigeons could travel somewhat faster than Jennifer since they did not need to move tangled branches out of the way as she did. Every now and then she would lose sight of them. She would look painstakingly at the loose dirt to find little footprints to guide her. When she turned right or left she would glimpse the resolute birds as they stood waiting patiently for her to catch up.

Finally after plodding along in this manner four or five minutes, Jennifer noticed the pudgy pigeons just standing still by what seemed to be only a pile of leaves. They began to scratch furiously with their bony feet as she gradually approached them. Under the moist leaves Jenny could see a hole lined with twigs and grasses. It was perhaps six feet across and two feet deep. The whole group of pigeons bowed together as if to say, "Help yourself to anything here."

Jennifer warily looked into the shallow hole and saw an assortment of rubbish. She would hardly call any of it treasures. She thought she would probably not be able to find anything of use in this absurd collection of junk.

There were twisted pieces of colored yarn, small balls of many types, and broken bottles which had once contained perfume or soda. Piles of torn magazines that had clearly been trampled lay open to crumpled and windblown pages. These papers covered wrappers of candy bars of many brands and other waste items.

As Jenny stepped down into the shallow pit, she felt a fluttering movement near her right ear. Tiger had caught up with her. Perched on her shoulder, he said, "Sorry I missed you, Jenny. When I woke

up I had a craving for a taste of the sweet nectar from those beautiful yellow flowers. I'll help you look for something useful here."

"That's great, Tiger." Jenny grinned at him and began to explore.

Sifting through the messy pile with her slim fingers, Jenny also found discarded items such as an old woman's fuzzy slipper, a filthy blue baby bib, an old black record, and a few pieces of gold costume jewelry that could not have been worth much. She recognized many other things similar to those that she had seen lying on the littered streets and side-walks near her house.

Feeling frustrated and helpless, Jennifer started to scramble back out of the hole when a pink plastic bottle caught her eye. Picking it up and examining it, Jenny was very excited suddenly. The drained bottle still contained a small amount of soap.

"Tiger, look what I found!"

It was an old bottle of bubble blowing solution much like the type which she had been using yesterday. Now Jennifer really did believe that the benevolent birds had true treasures on their island. Her only hope was that the sparse solution was not too little or too stale. She needed to be able to blow a bubble large enough to carry her back to her parents.

The unselfish pigeons had been regarding Jenny closely while she fingered their cluttered riches.

They were very generous and did not seem at all bothered as she picked up piece after piece of their belongings. They noticed that Jennifer's face had brightened when she spotted the bubble bottle.

The friendly pigeons cackled among themselves as they watched Jenny turning the simple bottle over in her hands. She was shaking it to listen to the solution slosh. They could feel her agitation and began flapping their wings restlessly to encourage her. Jenny did not forget her manners. She spoke to the inquisitive birds when she once more stood on the trampled grass near the treasure nest.

"Please, can I take this bottle back to the clearing to show the peacock? I think it is exactly what I need to help me leave your island. I would be forever grateful to you for sharing the contents with me. You really have found some amazing treasures on your flights to our cities. Thank you for letting me hunt through them."

Seven
The Owls' Advice

As if answering Jennifer, the nodding pigeons instantly began to march back through the prickly underbrush. They turned every minute or so to assure themselves that Jenny was following them. It seemed to Jenny that the return walk took longer than the previous hike to the treasure next. She did not know if this was because she was anxious to show the peacock her incredible find or because return trips always seem to be longer and more boring.

The weary group finally reached the grassy clearing where an ample breakfast had been set out for Jennifer. She had been noticing her stomach growling as she kept her eyes on the twisting path and her friendly guides. The wise peacock had again seemed to read Jenny's mind. An enormous platter of fluffy pancakes smothered in strawberries and whipped cream was set on a yellow brocade cloth. The guiding peacock spread one of its wings in the direction of the enticing food. Jenny immediately sat down to enjoy the scrumptious meal.

The young girl giggled when she saw Tiger already settled on a nearby porcelain plate. Teasingly she said, "Tiger, I should have known you would beat me here for breakfast. These pancakes look as yummy as the ones my mother makes me on weekend mornings."

Jennifer's mind began to wander back home to thoughts of her absent parents. Salty tears filled her wistful eyes as she told Tiger, "My mother has been so ill the past few months. How can I help my parents when I'm so far away?"

Tiger replied, "Don't worry. We'll help them together."

Having finished her stack of golden pancakes, Jenny sipped her fresh orange juice. She composed in her mind some words to ask the tolerant peacock for help.

Holding up the bottle of soap solution, she said, "Dear peacock, I have enjoyed very much these days that I have spent on your island. If I was not so worried about my mother, I might like to stay with you longer. I am concerned about my mother and she must be anxious about me. I would like to give my mother some of your special nourishment. If it gives you strength, maybe it would make my mother stronger too. I want her to regain her health."

The fatherly peacock smiled amiably at Jennifer. "Of course I cannot promise you what the results of the spring water might be. We will direct you to the distant cave though. Only the wise owls know of its concealed location. They describe the route to all the chosen envoys."

It continued, "After the mysterious trip is completed, the chosen one automatically forgets the spring's location. He also cannot remember the covert directions that he has been given. Follow this pebbled path to the owls' roost. They will have a meeting with you."

The royal bird then indicated a shaded path that led through some red azalea bushes. It wound deeper into the midst of some evergreen trees.

Jennifer felt very small again as she wandered along this deserted path to the owls' roost. She had glimpsed many owls during her stay on the island. There were barn owls, snowy owls, hawk owls, and eagle owls. She had noticed other kinds which she could not name, asleep in tall trees. They were all very handsome, but Jenny preferred the snowy owls to all the others.

Tiger broke into her thoughts at this point. He hovered over the top of her head. Jennifer could feel a slight movement of his little legs entangled in her glossy hair.

She questioned him, "Where have you been? Did you finally get enough to eat? For such a little insect, you sure have a big appetite."

"Well, I really think I could have nibbled a little more, but I wanted to hear what the owls have to say," he said. "When will you see them?"

Answering Tiger, Jennifer pointed to a huge evergreen tree directly in front of them. It was the daytime shelter for many of the sleepy owls. Jenny could see a snowy owl sitting dramatically on one of the sturdy branches. It posed beautifully since its white feathers contrasted with the dark green foliage. She was fond of this type of owl because it did not have horns on its head like some of the others. Jenny had learned that the tufts of feathers on their heads were not really horns. Still, she thought the scruffy tufts made some of the varieties of owls look mean.

Jenny sensed what seemed to be hundreds of gawking eyes watching her as she approached the shadowy tree. She told her loyal friend, "Tiger, I'm worried about asking the owls for help."

"But, Jenny," he tried to assure her, "you need to find the hidden spring. They are the only ones who can tell you what you need to know."

Right away, a soft, deep hoot welcomed them. Jennifer speedily spotted a magnificent eagle owl that had made the rumbling sound. It hooted dramatically in bursts of long and short tones.

"I can understand what it is saying to me, Tiger!" she announced. "It's strange, but the hoots sound like a Morse code language. My father taught me Morse code last summer. We would play fun games of leaving messages for one another on my tape recorder. Isn't it great that the code that I learned can come in handy now?"

The advising butterfly flapped down to Jenny's shoulder and warned, "Yes, but you'd better listen. The owl is ready to speak."

The eagle owl sternly explained to Jennifer that the owls would only tell her the instructions to the faraway cave one time. She must remember each step and follow it accurately. The alert owls had heard from the unselfish pigeons that Jenny had found more bubble solution. Knowing that she would be traveling in the air, the eagle owl cautioned her about strong winds and air currents.

After these strict warnings, the eagle owl stepped back farther into the dense branches and the snowy owl continued. With more hoots and a few shrieks for emphasis, it described the confusing route that Jennifer must take.

"You must leave our island going east. Float eastward until you are able to see the undeniable outline of an island that is shaped like a tarantula. You should be able to count eight peninsulas attached to the nucleus. As you fly over the center of the island where all the legs join together, change your direction to north. This first part of the extended journey might take as long as three hours. You will be depending on a steady breeze to blow you, not on wings which would speed your journey."

The owl proceeded, "After turning northward, you will hopefully float five or six hours until you can see a giant island. It seems to be continuously burning. There is an active volcano directly in the erupting center. The strong winds around the area always blow the towering flames and blinding ashes northward. In addition to smothering ashes, the volcano also belches pieces of popcorn high into the smoky sky. You will know that this is the correct volcanic island if you can hear the sound of popping corn when you approach."

At this time, the snowy owl became very noisy with its screeching. "Don't attempt to save time by flying over the top of the volcano. It will be impossible to float over the volcano without the heat bursting your bubble. Skirt around the circumference of the exploding island. Go far enough away from the blast before you resume your correct direction."

The intelligent owl warned, "It will be very dangerous for you. The height that the exploding particles reach is always changing. You will be very busy guiding your delicate bubble out of harm's way. Once you can continue in a northward course, rest for awhile. The next direction change will be about six hours from the hazardous volcano. That time limit is a mere guess. We have never directed someone who cannot fly before. Flying is definitely faster than drifting in a bubble."

The hawk owl now interrupted the snowy owl. He told Jenny, "Even though you must rest, you need to be looking for your next course marker. Listen for a thunderous waterfall. It will be found on a picturesque island that is covered with millions of gorgeous, richly colored flowers. You will hear the deafening waterfall from miles away. Then you will begin to perceive the wonderful beauty from the sky. You will also be able to distinctly smell the strong aroma of apple pie. Don't set your bubble down here though. You must control it to float eastward again for a few hours."

Finishing these specific directions, the fussy owl cautioned, "On the last leg of your journey you must remain awake to spot the tiny island where you will be landing. The island resembles a banana from the sky. You will not make it out though until you have passed most of the island. Turn around to see it from behind. It will take much skill to time a final landing before you are too far past the island and over the water. I can tell you one thing that might help you to see the island in time. The air around the island seems to make it look blue."

Eight
A Sparrow's Help

The hawk owl was abruptly silent. Jennifer could hear nothing in the evergreen tree. She listened to the symphony of birds chirping noisily in the other parts of the island. Only quiet surrounded her. There were no more hoots or screeches. It was as if the numerous owls had sticky tape keeping their sharp beaks closed tightly.

Jenny was a little confused about the island of flowers. She asked the snowy owl, "Can you please describe the flower island to me again?"

As the learned owls had warned her though, they only gave her the puzzling directions once. Not one of the reserved owls offered to repeat anything.

Frustrated, Jennifer turned to look at Tiger, "I think we need to leave now. I am anxious to talk to the peacock." Tiger nodded and fluttered his wings. He left Jenny's shoulder and flew swiftly on ahead of her.

The baffled girl found the narrow path easily. While she pushed the bothersome branches out of the way, she reflected on the bewildering instructions that she had been given. She dreaded making the lengthy trip to the hidden cave, but she knew she must go.

The kingly peacock had remained in the peaceful clearing waiting for her while she spoke to the superior owls. It fanned its beautiful white and black plumage as Jenny neared it. As it had happened so many times before, the solemn bird communicated to the confused girl without opening its narrow beak.

"Did you listen well to the owls?"

"I did listen carefully to them," Jennifer replied, "but I am a little worried. I may not be able to find the correct turning points. Worse yet, I am afraid that I may not be able to make the bubble go where I want it to go. When I came to your island I did not direct the bubble. It just seemed to know where to go. It floated like an apple blossom on the breeze."

The vigilant peacock chuckled at her concerns. It assured Jennifer, "Everything will be okay. It is easy to make your bubble change directions. All you need to do is blow on the inside walls of the orb in the direction of the way which you want to move. Believe me, that will be the simplest problem that you will need to solve. You are a bright girl. I know that if you were paying attention to the owls when they spoke, you will not forget the necessary markers."

Now the splendid bird waved its gorgeous wing. This impressive motion alerted all the birds that had gathered in the grassy ring to form a large circle around Jennifer. She understood it was time to begin her solitary trip.

Curtsying low to the unique peacock, she said, "Thank you for your wonderful hospitality. I had never before imagined such a place as this. I am glad that you chose me to retrieve your prized vase. I will never forget my visit here. I hope that you will not forget me."

Jennifer tugged the bottle of soap solution from her jeans pocket. She held it in one hand and unscrewed the cap with the other. She fingered the flimsy wand slowly. Calmly Jenny pulled it out of the bottle even though her heart was racing. She was very excited to know if the soap solution was still capable of making strong bubbles.

The round loop at the end of the plastic wand was full of soap film. Jennifer blew gently on it as she had always done before. The soap bulged out an inch from the ring but would not grow larger. The tiny bubble popped and sprayed Jenny's lips with bitter soap. She tried again and the same thing happened. Once more she attempted to enlarge the bubble, but it only broke.

Jennifer looked to the remarkable peacock for help, but it had its back to her. The other birds which had been watching began to chatter and squawk. She was puzzled and thought it was futile to blow anymore.

Suddenly Jenny heard a steady flapping in the air above her head. She watched one lone sparrow

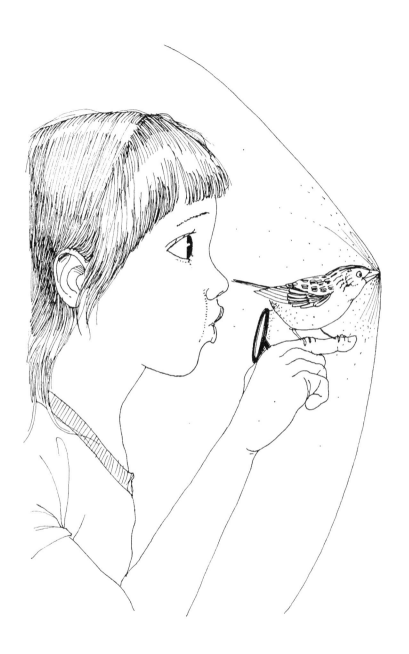

coming toward her. Boldly holding out her pointer finger, the agile little bird landed on it. It curled its tiny claws tightly around her finger as if it were a thin branch. The brown bird could not have weighed even an ounce. It slid down toward Jenny's palm as far as it could go, but she was still able to manipulate the soap wand.

Jennifer puffed on the soap film softly. The nimble sparrow touched the bubble gently with its sharp beak. It seemed to have magically pulled the soap film to a roomy size around the young girl. With the spry sparrow still clinging firmly to her hand, the bubble grew bigger and bigger with air from Jenny's warm breath.

Within a minute, Jennifer found herself and her new companion completely surrounded within a colorless orb. She could hear the confident peacock outside the clear sphere reminding her, "You must remember that it is not always necessary to be large to be successful. Just as the small sparrow was able to help you, you have been able to aid others. You will be able to accomplish much as a child."

Nine
Hurricane Trouble

As Jennifer listened to the grateful peacock recalling her usefulness, the glistening sphere began to rise off the bumpy ground. She could see some of the interested birds watching her from the clearing while others such as the sage owls remained in their secluded trees. They were all keeping their feathered heads turned toward her. She immediately realized that she had left without Tiger. She screamed, "Tiger, where are you?"

At this instant Jenny saw the devoted butterfly circling hopefully in the clearing below. It was impossible to return for him. She heard the dependable peacock say, "Don't worry. We'll take good care of Tiger. We will treat him always as an honored guest for your sake."

While she sadly waved to Tiger, Jennifer's shining bubble rose higher and higher. Now the throngs of birds on the isolated island looked as small as grains of pepper. Some of the frisky birds, such as the sparrows and hummingbirds, escorted her for awhile. Jenny honestly remarked to the tiny sparrow who shared her bubble, "It's so nice to have your friends guiding us. They are flapping their wings so hard that I don't need to blow on the inside of the bubble to direct us eastward."

Nodding its tiny head, the talented sparrow said, "They want to help you as much as they can. We all think you are very brave and special to us."

On this first leg of her dubious journey, Jenny made up her mind to stay alert and observant. She did not want to miss the first island that she needed to locate. It was not hard to remain awake because she was so edgy. The energetic hummingbirds were circling her now in a flurry as if in a final farewell. Jennifer watched them as they turned back to the birds' island. She was glad to have the talkative sparrow for pleasant company since its companions had already begun their return flight.

"Dear sparrow," she said glumly, "we are all alone in this enormous sky. Thank you for helping me form this sphere. Please tell me your name."

"I am called Dusty because I am so lightweight," announced the sparrow. "I'm proud to accompany you on your journey."

"You're really kind to offer to help me," Jennifer replied. "I know you will be aiding me again. Right now we need to pay attention to our course. I don't want to miss the tarantula-shaped island. That is my first marker."

Every minute now Jennifer needed to puff on the inside of her translucent bubble to keep it floating eastward. Her cheeks were tired of blowing at the end of an hour. Thankfully, a constant breeze then picked up the bouncing orb and carried it along.

Relieved, Jenny confided to Dusty, "It's nice to have a light wind so I can rest and watch the ocean splashing beneath us."

Dusty agreed, "Yes, I'm afraid that I cannot blow hard enough to really help you move much."

"That's okay," Jennifer reassured him. "At this speed I can actually have the chance to see large fish swimming near the surface of the dark water. They look so graceful. Sometimes I can even see a grey dolphin rise slightly out of the water and then dive back down."

Time passed peacefully now for Jenny and she began to think how easy it was to travel this way.

Unexpectedly there was a harsh push on the frail bubble as if an enormous hand had come from the sky to give it a rough shove. Of course there was nothing there. Jennifer realized that parts of the vast sky had grown dark and mean. The strong push she had felt was a brisk wind that had come from nowhere. It had felt like a thrust and a tug at the same time.

Jenny regarded the brilliant sun to make certain that she stayed on course. When she looked behind her she could see a frightening funnel cloud approaching her at a rapid speed.

"Dusty, look at the clouds behind us!" she shouted. "I think we may soon be in trouble. Those rolling clouds can be terribly dangerous."

Dusty tried to relieve her fears by commenting, "Sometimes tornadoes can be good. One of them brought me to the bird island last year."

Jennifer still felt totally perplexed. She was being pushed so hard that she could not have turned the sphere even if she did know in which direction to go. The rotating funnel closed in on the lone bubble. Jenny had the helpless sensation of being spun around and around.

After a few minutes of this spinning Jennifer was really feeling dizzy. She thought she could not remain in the disabled bubble any longer. Just then, the twirling motion stopped. There was silence and calm all around her.

"Dusty, are you okay?" Jenny asked. "I don't know how you stayed on my finger through all that spinning."

"It was difficult," the faint bird answered. "Where did the wind go? I can't hear any swishing sounds around us."

Jennifer didn't answer because she was staring directly below her. There were tall palm trees covering parts of an island and narrow tan beaches outlining the rest. In every direction Jenny could see long sections of land leading out to the endless ocean.

These peninsular sections were surrounded on every side by water except the side that was attached to the center of the island. Now Jennifer realized that the twister cloud had brought her over the middle of the tarantula-shaped island. To be certain, she counted eight peninsulas as the shrewd owls had described.

"Dusty," Jenny shouted excitedly, "how nice it is to find ourselves at this spot! I know why there was such a turbulent windstorm followed by such calm. I remember studying about weather in school. The funnel cloud was not a tornado, it was a hurricane."

"I believe you, but why is it so quiet now?" wondered Dusty.

Jennifer explained, "When we were being pushed and pulled, the sphere must have been inside the wall clouds. They surround the eye of the destructive hurricane. At the moment we are within the center of these wall clouds where there are no winds and no rain. The air will be calm for a time. It will probably only stay peaceful for less than an hour."

Even now Jenny was beginning to feel a slight tugging which became more and more fierce. She sighed, "How can we compete with these stormy winds to turn our bubble toward the north as the owls told me I must?"

The apprehensive sparrow didn't answer. Its toes were gripping Jenny's finger like a clamp to be ready for the wild gusts again.

Jennifer remembered the convincing peacock's last words to her. He reminded her that even though she was small, she was capable of many things. She decided, "I think we should just let these winds take us where they want. Maybe we can turn the bubble after it is released from the wall clouds."

Dusty replied weakly, "I don't think I can hold your finger as tightly as I did before. I'm tired."

"Don't worry," Jenny said confidently, "I'll help you. All we have to do is stay inside the orb. At least we are protected from the cold and wind."

Jennifer then cautiously sat down, tucking her feet and hands tightly to her body. This seemed to be the best idea so that she would not puncture the bubble and fall into the roiling storm. She leaned down to cover Dusty with her head and shoulders. Snuggled there, they patiently waited for the whirling clouds to free them.

With a sudden surge of air Jenny's bubble popped out of the chaotic clouds. It reminded her of watermelon seeds being spit onto the ground by playful children. Lifting her head, the exhausted girl said, "Look at the sunshine, Dusty! It's all around us."

The retreating clouds were disappearing into the eastern sky as quickly as they had come. By observing the position of the sun in the sky, Jennifer discerned that she was now floating southward. She began to puff as hard as she could to rotate the traveling bubble northward. Her strained cheeks were sore and her breath was gone when finally she scooted the quivering orb into a breeze. It picked up the vulnerable sphere and took her gently toward the north.

Jenny admitted to Dusty, "I need sleep—a lot of sleep. This hurricane has really tired me. I don't think I can blow even one more time."

She remained curled up in the middle of the bubble. Jennifer closed her droopy eyelids as she drifted along on the soothing breeze. Dusty did not move. They both fell asleep quickly. Jenny simply could not stay awake to watch for the volcano island. After all, while the comforting wind carried her, there was not much to do.

Ten
Popcorn

Jennifer dreamed that she was falling, falling, faster and faster. She could not recall where she had been and what was causing her to drop. She knew she was scared though. Suddenly she awakened from her dream to see that she really was falling, not fast, but slowly heading down to the water.

Standing up quickly, Jennifer woke up Dusty with a start, "I'm sorry Dusty but I have to blow on the bubble! I have to make it rise again! When we went to sleep the water was a great distance from us. The tarantula island seemed from the sky to be the size of a dinner plate. Now the ocean is rushing up to meet us. I'm really worried."

Dusty flew to the top of the bubble suggesting, "Maybe if I flap my wings up here it will help."

Jenny nodded her head while she kept puffing. The foamy bubbles in her bath water at home popped when they touched the side of the bathtub or the warm water. She knew as soon as the doomed orb touched the pounding waves it would burst.

Jennifer could swim, but how far would she get? How long could she float without becoming exhausted and needing to get out of the water? She didn't ask Dusty, but she knew that sparrows can't swim. What would become of him?

As she floated downward, Jennifer noticed a large grey whale swimming just under the surface of the green water. She noticed the whale's fluke rising up and down gracefully as it swam. It was going in the same direction as Jenny's sphere was proceeding.

Jennifer was close enough now to see the two blowholes on the top of its head. She noted along its lower back that there were some low humps near the enormous tail. Since whales have poor eyesight and most cannot smell, she was not fearful that the whale would try to harm her. What would happen though if her bubble burst accidentally right in front of the gaping mouth?

"Dusty," she cried, "do you see the whale? If it is a baleen whale, we will not be taken into its mouth. The stiff baleen only strains very small animals from the ocean. But what if the whale has teeth?"

Dusty looked alarmed and flapped his wings even faster.

Jenny consoled him by recounting her limited knowledge of whales. "I remember that my science teacher told my class that two blowholes on the top of a whale's head means the whale is a kind of baleen whale. There are two blowholes on this whale. Now that we're closer, I can see white blotches of barnacles on its tough skin. It must be a grey whale. That's good."

"But Jennifer," Dusty doubtfully said, "we still will sink into the water and I can't swim."

Jenny now heard a hissing sound like steam being released from an aluminum pipe. She watched wordlessly while a cloud of water vapor was blown out of the top of the whale's huge head. The misty spout of water grew higher and higher. As the massive whale moved forward, the vapor jet caught the little girl's bubble and forced it up into the sky. It actually was an exceptionally hard spurt.

"Dusty, do you see? This gigantic whale must have known that we needed help. It blew us up into the sky! We're going to be okay."

The little bird stopped beating his wings to joyfully take a needed rest on Jenny's wrist. Wondering what would happen next, Jennifer studied the dark water. She understood the reason for the whale's lengthy stay on the surface of the ocean. The tremendous whale was a cow. Jenny guessed that she had been waiting for her young calf to swim up close to its mother's side.

"What a cute picture it is to see such a mammoth whale swimming along with a much smaller baby traveling by her side!" Jennifer exclaimed. The devoted whale began to dive and Jenny soon lost sight of them.

Dusty barely murmured, "Yes, I see." He was so weak his eyes were tightly closed. Jennifer let him sleep and just watched the swaying water silently. The wayward bubble was drifting now on a lazy draft that carried the shiny orb in a northerly direction.

Jennifer was beginning to feel very hungry. It seemed as if she had left the island of the birds days ago. Her last meal had been the savory pancakes and strawberry breakfast. Now, for some strange reason, she had a considerable craving for fresh popcorn with plenty of butter and salt on it.

Every Friday night at home Jenny's father made delicious hot popcorn as a celebration of the weekend. Her mouth began to water and her empty stomach begged for food as it growled continuously. Just wishing for food was not going to help Jennifer. How could she find something to eat in the middle of the bare sky over the ocean?

At the moment Jennifer was not only daydreaming of popcorn but smelling it too. She definitely heard a popping sound that grew louder and louder. The nonstop noise woke up her friend.

"Dusty, can you hear that loud racket? We're getting closer to it," Jenny yelled.

Dusty sleepily asked, "What is it?"

"I don't know, but we're floating toward it," Jennifer replied.

Off in the distance Jenny could barely discern a volcanic island. From where she was, she could only see great puffs of smoke rising over the top of the immense mountain. Jennifer remembered what the incredible owls had told her about a dangerous volcano. They had prepared her to skirt it in order to remain on the correct course. The stubborn breeze that she was riding was carrying her closer and closer every minute to this erupting mountain.

Approaching it, Jenny shouted, "The exploding volcano is a cinder cone! It's amazing! Instead of sizzling cinders being released from the central vent, there is pungent popcorn falling all around the cone."

"Jennifer, I've never seen anything like this before," said Dusty. "The piles of popcorn look tasty!"

The serious owls had vigorously warned Jenny about traveling over the very top of the unpredictable volcano, but she was really famished. She wished, "I sure would like to eat a handful or two of popcorn. I bet it's great!"

Thinking aloud, Jennifer said, "How will we be able to get close enough to the exploding popcorn to reach out for some? If we fly over the vent we'll be rocketed into the sky by a burst of hot air. If we do somehow manage to skirt the heat vent, how can we gather any popcorn without breaking our protective bubble?"

The dazed sparrow shook his head dejectedly and shrugged his shoulders.

"Wait, I have an idea!" whooped Jenny.

She began huffing on the perilous bubble as hard as she could to force it to turn eastward. Time was getting short so she puffed on the clear bubble wall in steady blows. She only took time to fill her lungs, blow, fill her lungs again, and blow. She kept a steady stream of air pressing on the inside of the sphere.

Now that she was situated on the east side of the rounded cone, Jennifer was aware of hot air being forced upward into the sky. She could plainly hear the whistling sound that it made. Where she was floating though, she could not actually feel the warm air. She was not afraid of being hit by popping kernels. Very calmly Jenny blew on the bottom of the sparkling orb. She desperately wanted to make it land very lightly on the mounds of popcorn that covered the inclined slope of the rumbling volcano.

Gently, very gently, Jennifer successfully touched the slippery bubble to the pieces of popcorn. Over and over she delicately bounced the soap bubble on the tilted slope until the bottom of the bubble was dusted with puffed corn. Luckily the bubble did not rupture. The bumpy popcorn was stuck fast to the pliable orb because of the sticky solution that formed it.

Proud of herself, Jenny asked, "There, Dusty, do you think I've collected enough popcorn? If we take too much, the bubble might burst from the added weight."

Dusty assured her, "That's plenty. I don't eat much."

Puffing now on the east side of the wet sphere again, Jennifer directed it away from the blasting volcano. She hoped to get at least a half mile away from the central vent. She feared a dreadful fall into the chamber where all the hot air and eruptions formed.

After continuous huffing for what seemed to be about fifteen minutes, Jenny could not resist the nagging temptation any longer. She wanted to try eating a piece of tempting popcorn.

She was happily satisfied, "Look, Dusty, the popcorn cooled. It's been on the outside of the sphere for awhile. It slowly worked itself through the soap solution and onto the inside bottom of the orb. Taste it, Dusty."

Dusty nibbled on one fluffy kernel while Jenny hungrily gobbled piece after piece until she was full. Once they were finished, they still had enough popcorn left to fill a small bucket, if they had one.

Sighing with satisfaction, Jennifer grinned saying, "It's time that we changed directions."

She started to push the bubble with her buttery breaths once again to get oriented in a northern direction. She was having a difficult time recalling what marker she was told to identify after she passed the popcorn volcano.

Eleven
Quilt Code

Heading northward now on a pulsing stream of air, Jennifer felt confused. The pinkish sun was beginning to set in the west and she was yawning often. Last night she had slept in the comfy nest of down feathers on the birds' island. Tonight it seemed that she would sleep with only her new friend in the silent darkness and her confining orb surrounding her.

"I miss my parents, Dusty," Jenny sighed. "I wish I was home in my own bed."

Dusty knowingly agreed, "Yes, home is always best, but maybe you'll be there tomorrow."

Jennifer understood that while she slumbered the air current which transported her might lead her astray. She definitely needed to close her eyes though.

She told Dusty, "You know, it really does not matter whether I stay awake or go to sleep. I don't know how to look at the stars to find directions anyway. Do you know about astronomy?"

Dusty offered wisely, "No, Jennifer, I think we have to trust that the air current will continue to carry us until morning. We will be able to change directions then if we are blown off course in the dark."

Jennifer settled down carefully in the bottom of the tranquil bubble and folded her legs up under her. She was not chilly because the homey sphere always seemed to insulate her from cold or heat.

"I'm so glad that you are with me, Dusty. I would be so lonely without you. Do you want to come sit on my legs?"

The comforting brown sparrow immediately flew to Jenny's pants and fluffed its silky feathers.

Jennifer confided, "I hope my poor parents aren't too worried that I'm gone. I just hope all this traveling to get to the mystical spring is worthwhile. I want to help. Do you think they'll believe me when I tell them about my adventures?"

"It will be hard for them, Jennifer, but they know you I'm sure. I'm sure they will believe that you are telling the truth," Dusty reassured her.

Jenny could readily imagine them with their mouths open, listening to her unbelievable story in shocked silence. Maybe she shouldn't tell them, maybe she should tell them, maybe she shouldn't tell them. She could not decide. With this dilemma on her troubled mind she fell asleep.

A bright yellow light was shining all around her when she awoke the next morning. By now Jennifer was accustomed to waking up inside her sheltering sphere. She did not have to remind herself where she was.

Jenny softly called, "Dusty, we're on the right course. Look at the sun!"

Since this morning sun was not rising in front of her, Jenny realized that she had not been forced eastward during the restful night. The warm sun was glowing to the right of her. She had been adrift on an air current that was taking her northward. Jennifer knew that she needed to go north, but she could not remember why.

Jenny tenderly lifted Dusty off her stiff legs and placed him on her cramped hand. While she stretched her arms she stood up inside the glimmering bubble to get a better view of the vast ocean around her. Off to the left of her she could glimpse what seemed to be a floating cloth. In fact, the strange object seemed to be many cloths of different colors just lying on top of the boundless water. It looked similar to her grandmother's large bed quilt that contained pieces of cotton cloth in hundreds of contrasting prints.

Jennifer's dependable orb lazily floated closer to the fantastic quilt. She could discern that it was not made out of fabric scraps at all.

"Dusty, look at that queer material down there in the water," Jenny pointed. "It looks sort of leathery."

Dusty suggested, "I've seen that odd type of thing before. Look closely."

Jennifer's observation revealed that this peculiar quilt was actually eight octopi of varied colors joined together.

"I studied octopi one summer at science camp," she explained. "We learned that when an octopus is excited it can change its color. It can be blue, brown, purple, red, yellow, white, or even striped."

Dusty answered, "You're right. I'm sure that is what we are seeing—octopi."

These sea animals were each a different color. All were floating on the water with their flat mantles shaped like pie wedges.

"I can't see any of the octopi's eight tentacles and none of the suction spots on their flowing legs," Jennifer stated. "Altogether they look like a pie cut into eight pieces. It reminds me to watch for the island that smells like apple pie. The owls informed me there was a plunging waterfall and gorgeous flowers there too."

No sooner had Jenny remembered these crucial details of her course than the clinging octopi broke their unusual formation. They disappeared in a dark spray of concealing ink. The young girl turned in every direction in order to focus on their manner of swimming away. They were nowhere in sight.

Jennifer questioned Dusty, "Do you think they were in this silly position just for me? Now that they accomplished their task, I think they have vanished to the ocean floor."

"Once an octopus draws water into its body, it can squeeze it back out. It can propel itself backward amazingly fast," Dusty said. "Aren't we lucky they were here when we needed them?"

The amusing octopi were not the only ones who were moving promptly. Jennifer's hovering orb had again been caught up on a swiftly blowing draft. She was skimming high above the expanse of saltwater very rapidly. In fact, this was no breeze. This was a strong gust from the south.

In the distance Jenny could see what seemed to be another extraordinary island looming into view. There was a misty appearance to it. It looked as though it was being sprayed with a water hose.

The bobbing bubble was blown closer to the island very quickly. Jennifer could now see that this unusual island was more colorful than she could ever have imagined.

"Dusty, look at all the bright flowers," she gasped. "I can see yellow, pink, orange, white, violet, and red colors speckled all over the rainbow island."

"I've never seen a prettier bouquet of blossoms, Jenny."

Jennifer breathed in deeply. She affirmed, "I smell fresh-baked apple pie. Mmmm! It smells just like our kitchen does when I come home from school or playing sometimes. My mother loves to bake."

There was not time to daydream about home though. The swift south wind was propelling them right into the damaging path of a noisy waterfall. It was cascading over a rocky cliff and could pull them down too.

The coarse splashes from the stunning waterfall would certainly also be hard enough to burst the bubble if Jenny could not steer them off course for a time. She blew frantically with all her might on the eastern side of the bubble. It was no use. The wind was really strong, too strong for the inexperienced girl to fight.

Jennifer did not give up though. She remembered the trusting peacock's faith in her. Bravely she said, "I'm going to blow the sphere down and under the pounding waterfall. That's the only way we can go. Help me, Dusty."

Summoning her strength, Jenny puffed on the bottom of the bubble in short quick bursts of breath. Dusty flapped his wings energetically. They made slow progress toward the back of the waterfall. The jagged boulders over which it was wildly tumbling were close enough to touch.

Jennifer's vague plan was to go between the crashing waterfall and the vertical mountainside. She would have to be careful not to float too close to the protruding rocks. They would surely pop the fragile sphere.

Arriving at the tunnel made by the falling water, Jenny's bubble bounced around. It was being pushed by the stirring air that was being disturbed by sprays of water. Thunderous claps of water struck the side of the bluff and the large stones in the rushing river below.

Because of all the restrictions on the airflow under the toppling falls, Jennifer's bubble was slowed immediately. It lost the south wind altogether. Bobbing up and down under the splattering waterfall, the sphere lazily floated out from the narrow passage.

Emerging from this spray, Jenny was thoroughly astonished at the splendor of the assortment of flowers displayed on the mountain.

Catching her breath, she said, "I wish I had my sunglasses. The colors are so bright now that I can see them up close! It almost hurts my eyes to stare at such glowing beauty."

The pigments in the rainbow were mirrored in the flower petals. Their blinding brightness was magnified to the highest power.

The appealing temptation to land her bubblecraft in the midst of this stunning bouquet was almost too great for Jennifer to repel. How delighted she would be to pick such breathtaking beauty!

"Dusty, I might never see such a wonder again, but it would be foolish to stop here. I might never find a way to return home again."

The mindful sparrow cautioned her, "You can't even think of landing! Your bubble is too fragile."

"You're right, Dusty. There isn't enough soap solution in the bottle to form a bubble on this island

and also on the island of the spring," Jenny concluded.

Sighing deeply, Jennifer thought about the last direction that the counseling owls had given her. Now she must turn her sphere eastward for the final step of her tiresome journey to the banana-shaped island. With one huge breath Jenny shut her eyes firmly and blew toward the east.

Twelve
Flying Fish Game

Weariness overcame Jennifer. Her flushed cheeks were tired of blowing. They felt very sore when she examined them with her fingertips. Not only were her weakened cheeks hurting, but her scratchy throat was extremely dry. Once she had eaten her fill of the abundant salted popcorn she had felt thirsty. The excitement of seeing the bizarre octopi and the spectacular waterfall had temporarily made her forget that her throat was parched. Now though, Jenny was beginning to feel desperate for a cold, quenching drink.

"I'm so thirsty, Dusty. Where will we able to find some water? My throat feels so dry. It's hard to talk. You must need some too by now," Jennifer declared.

Dusty agreed, "Yes, I do, but even if we are able to locate water, how will we be able to bring it into the sphere without breaking the protective wall?"

Jennifer answered weakly, "I don't know, Dusty. I'm so tired."

For the first time since she had left her home and her parents, Jennifer sat down and dabbed tears from her eyes with the corner of her crimson blouse. Immediately, when she ceased blowing on the bubble, it began to abruptly descend. Jenny was not forgetting what she had to do to keep herself up in the air. She just was exhausted. She could not puff even one more time.

Jennifer wiped her watering eyes again, not to remove tears though. She was seeing something unnatural. Below her there seemed to be a flock of flashy dragonflies flying along the ocean surface. Each rainbow-colored insect was about as long as her arm. They were not merely in flight as she first thought. They seemed to be propelling themselves out of the green water. Then they glided for long distances before reentering the ocean.

Pointing to the dynamic water, Jenny asked Dusty, "Do you see those huge dragonflies? They are not just skimming over the waves. Watch them. They are diving in the water and then they jump out again."

Dusty nodded his little head and said, "I see them, Jennifer. How do they do that?"

Since her coasting sphere had floated downward, Jenny could observe these odd animals closely now. They were not humming dragonflies, but undeniably fish.

She decided, "They must be flying fish! Can you see the layers of shimmering scales on their sleek bodies? They do not have wings."

"It's remarkable!" Dusty replied. "They can use their powerful fins to glide so far."

Of course she could not measure precisely the length of their controlled vaults. Jennifer estimated though that some of them leaped a car length. Others seemed to fly half the length of a small house.

Because she was so entranced with the activities of the flying fish, Jenny's busy mind had not been on her bubble's descent. Suddenly the frothy ocean was two yards from her feet. Jennifer could do nothing but pinch her eyes closed and wait for the bottomless water to swallow her.

She shouted, "Hang on Dusty! We're going to hit the water."

Jenny did not feel a splash or a pop. She sensed she had been forcefully bumped up into the air. Before she could gasp for breath, she felt a sharp drive forward. Then there was a slick glide that lasted for a short time. This predictable series of a bump, then a thrust, and then a smooth slide happened again and again.

Jennifer opened her eyes wide after the initial bump. She was astonished to see that the flying fish were passing her supple sphere along the surface of the water as if it were a beach ball. Dusty was gripping her ring finger so tightly it was turning red.

It fascinated Jenny to watch how one fish would take her precious bubble on its back for a steady glide. Then, before it dived into the dark ocean, another energetic fish would jump out of the water.

They would connect just long enough to switch the orb from one back to another. The second one would fly under the bubble to take Jennifer farther. Their planned passes were accomplished so effortlessly that Jenny never felt a falling sensation. She only experienced the forward movement.

"Thank heavens, Dusty," Jennifer expressed gratefully. "We might not be floating in the correct direction, but I'm glad that these playful fish caught us. They won't let us fall."

Her simple words comforted Dusty so he relaxed his intense hold. "I just hope they don't stop their funny game suddenly and strand us," he remarked.

About two miles ahead of her, Jennifer could see a blue mist hanging in the clear sky. It was barely touching the rocking surface of the brimming ocean. Squinting her eyes did not help her see this blurry cloud any better. She kept her inquiring eyes fixed on it. The flying fish still continued their amusing prank. Jenny was lifted tenderly again and again. The blue cloud enveloped them now and the reliable fish kept carrying the fanciful orb.

Jenny glanced back over her shoulder often. All she could see was the blue mist surrounding her dependent sphere. Ahead of her she could see faint white light which meant that she would be emerging from the misty cloud. Still her surroundings were hidden.

Annoyed about this occurrence, Jennifer recalled how the prophetic owls had described the banana-shaped island to her. They had told her that there would be a blue mist hanging over it. Because of this hindering cloud she would not know the final island until it was almost too late. It happened!

Jenny had begun to pass the desolate island before she knew it. The mist was gone. Now she could see how the sandy shoreline of the island did indeed curve to resemble a banana.

Jennifer had to make a quick decision. She told Dusty, "This is where the spring is. We have to land close to the beach. We may need to pop the bubble to stop. Be ready to fly."

Dusty was concerned. He asked, "But Jenny, what about you? How will you get there?"

Jenny was so deep in thought she did not answer right away. There was a large boulder in the throbbing water directly in the path in which the flying fish were progressing. They were beginning to veer to the right in order to miss it. Jennifer began puffing as hard as she could to bump herself off the back of a flying fish.

After three large, deep breaths Jennifer realized that she was not strong enough to free herself by blowing. "I hoped to land the bubble on top of that boulder, Dusty. It's hopeless."

Determined not to allow the frolicking fish to bear her much farther, Jenny scratched the bottom of the traveling bubble with her fingernails. She was digging madly with her fingers just like a mole claws its way through dirt. And it worked! The soap sphere popped and Jennifer slid off the flying fish into the icy ocean.

Jennifer managed to keep her head above the murky water when she dropped those few feet. She gulped bitterly at the shock of the cold. Then immediately she began swimming with strong strokes toward the welcoming shore of the remote island. She guessed that she was about a football field's length from the shell-covered beach. That was a long distance to swim, but Jenny had no choice. There was nowhere else to go and she refused to think that she would not make it safely.

Thankfully, the diminishing waves were not too large and rough. In fact, the jostling waves were prodding Jennifer toward the land as though she was a piece of driftwood. While she floated, she attempted to see where Dusty had flown. He was nowhere in sight. She hoped he had not fallen into the devouring water. Had he been hurt when the falling bubble popped? Jenny had quit trying to swim by this time. Nothing she did made a difference. She was pushed and then floated out somewhat. She was shoved again and glided back a little and so on until the flowing whitecaps finally won the taxing contest they had with the ebbing waves. Jennifer reached out her arms to touch the fine sand.

Thirteen
The Cave Lady

Jennifer lay still on the moist beach for a few minutes. She knew that she was not injured. The bumpy waves had tossed her about though, so she was very weary. Her lanky arms were sore from her battling swim and the cool water lapped in rhythm over her motionless legs. Her drenched clothes clung to her damp skin and she had lost all her shoes and socks in the sea. Jenny's long brown hair was wrapped around her neck and resembled wet seaweed.

Feeling in her soaked jeans pocket with her right hand, Jennifer was distressed to discover that the soap bottle was gone. It must have been wrenched from her during the frustrating struggle to shore. She reasoned that even if she was able to uncover the spring of medicine, she would not be able to leave the uninhabited island. Jenny had planned to fly home, but now how would she get there? Who would help her?

The illuminating sun was setting fast and lonely night would soon surround her. There was no sign of Dusty. Jennifer realized that she must at least search for a simple shelter. Slowly standing, Jenny studied the treeless beach. There was no natural refuge there. If she merely reclined on the solitary beach in the wet sand, her damp clothing would be sure to give her a chill. Things could not be much more hopeless.

Jennifer was exhausted, shivering, and famished. She did not believe there was a plain solution to any of her distressing problems. Sighing gloomily, she decided to walk up onto the tan sand toward the lofty trees that were thick in the center of the uninviting island.

Using both hands to carefully spread the packed branches apart, Jenny gradually crept into the dreary forest. She clumsily stepped on one coarse rock after another with her bare feet and flinched each time. In addition to the sharp stones, there were masses of pine needles and tiny thorny branches lying all over the forest floor.

After hobbling for a short distance, Jennifer was relieved to identify a partially hidden opening to a cave. It was about fifty feet in front of her and to the right. She was always suspicious of dark places and she knew this would be no different. At least this paltry recess would offer her some escape from the nighttime chilliness. A persistent breeze had already begun to rustle the drooping branches of the trees overhead.

Luckily when she arrived at the edge of the obscure cave, Jenny spied a muddy carpet of green moss on the entrance floor. At least the dense moss would soften the rock floor so she could get a few hours of necessary sleep. Entering the dismal cave, she tiptoed in toward one wall. The rock wall would give her somewhere to rest her head and back.

It actually felt good to slump down and just let her tired arms drop to her side. Her strained legs began to twitch from the laborious swim followed by the painful trek through the woods. Jennifer was still very hungry and damp, but for the moment what she needed most was a safe spot to nap. She fell asleep quickly. But concern about the dreary cave and any animals that might inhabit it made her toss and turn with worry.

Before the sleepy sun had even begun to rise, Jenny awoke to a muffled shuffling sound. Opening her pinched eyes slowly, she blinked to accustom them to the dark. At the rear of the unlit cave she could barely see a blurry yellow light. It was the type of soft gleam which comes from a screened nightlight. It scarcely emitted a dainty circle of mellow light around itself. As Jennifer regarded the fuzzy glow, the soothing beacon seemed to be approaching her, but very deliberately. It only illuminated the area closest to itself which looked to be slightly pink colored.

Strangely, as this light beam moved toward her, Jenny was not frightened. In fact, she thought she was having a wonderful dream. She was calm, yet anxious to know what was bringing this revealing lamp to her.

Aroused now, Jennifer could distinguish a human form as it ambled closer and closer to her. The flickering light grew brighter and bigger. Jenny noted it was a rusty lantern being carried by a tall, slim woman dressed all in pastel pink.

The advancing woman was young, maybe only twenty years old. Her groomed head was crowned with plentiful, black, shoulder-length hair. It was combed sleek and straight to frame her attractive face. Her smooth complexion was very pale, almost white. She grinned at Jennifer with thin pink lips which seemed to have been flawlessly drawn on her mouth with a delicate colored pencil.

Jennifer shyly rose to meet this pretty lady who seemed to be a fabulous dream except that she smelled wonderfully like a carnation. Jenny had never sniffed anything in her dreams so she was convinced of the reality of this alluring woman.

The appealing woman looked down upon Jenny since she was a head and shoulders taller than the inquisitive girl. Smiling as she spoke, she welcomed Jennifer to the black cave.

She said, "I am so glad to see a human who has come from outside of this cave. It has been years since I have had a visitor such as you. Each year the needy birds dispatch an envoy to me to collect their essential liquid from my treasured spring. They are the only creatures I have had the opportunity to greet in at least fifty years."

Jenny was surprised to hear this from such a youthful lady. She wondered how she remained looking so young, but she was too polite to ask.

"The royal peacock has sent me to this island," Jennifer explained. "I helped the bird community three days ago. The golden eagle had recently withdrawn precious liquid from the spring on this island. He had unfortunately dropped it in a pool of water on his return. I retrieved the crystal vase for the dejected birds. In return, the thankful owls felt that they should give me the directions to find the fountain. I want to collect a small amount to take home."

Jennifer continued, "My mother is ill and I thought the exceptional liquid might be able to return her good health and make her strong as it does for the birds. I am sorry to disturb you. If you will indicate the way to the secret spring, I will be grateful."

"Of course I will guide you," consented the pink lady. "First let me provide you with food. You look extremely tired and you must be terribly hungry after your hazardous trip. You must tell me how you were able to venture such a long distance in only two days. I can see that you are wearing damp clothing. Surely you did not swim the whole way!"

The pretty lady turned to prepare some things for Jenny to eat. The little girl was astonished to see two beautiful, opaque wings on her back. They glistened and fluttered in the revealing light of the lantern.

Jennifer had not seen any food in the abandoned cave when she had entered it the evening before. She had not noticed anything edible by the dim walls this morning either. Within a moment the benevolent lady who Jenny thought must be a fairy turned toward her. She held a shiny silver platter piled with brown toast and grape jelly, a colorful fruit salad, some chocolate doughnuts, and glasses brimming with orange and apple juice.

Jenny only had a minute to wonder where all these treats had been hidden. The generous fairy set the polished tray at her bruised feet saying, "Please sit down and eat until you are full. When you are feeling better we can discuss your risky trip to my island and the way to the spring. It is not far from here."

Fourteen
Awful Discoveries

Jenny ate leisurely. Now she was not afraid to explore further into the gloomy cave. She was aware that the kind fairy would be with her. She wished for some time to just sit and relax, before taking off on this cave tour.

The lovely fairy regarded her while she ate, but did not bother her with any questions. When Jennifer was finished she wiped her sticky mouth properly with a puffy pink cloth that was lying on the serving tray. She smiled up at the nice woman who was standing near the cave entrance.

"Follow me, Jennifer," coaxed the eager fairy. "I will lead you to the spring of special nourishment."

The elegant fairy turned gracefully to walk into the depths of the soundless cave. Jenny marveled at the beauty of the shimmering wings on her straight back. The sheer wings were almost as long as the fairy was tall. They spread out on each side of her back like the petals of an open rose.

It was not troubling for Jennifer to pursue the capable woman into the musty dimness. The old lantern was lit and the sensible fairy held it high above her head. The tight walls of the tapering cavern were bright where the two of them walked. Jenny would turn now and then to look behind her. The daylight that had broken the night sky while she ate was no longer visible.

Darkness chased Jennifer and gulped down the path after her. She could touch each side of the close cave walls by stretching out both of her arms. This confined space would have certainly annoyed her if she had not been with such a thoughtful, reassuring fairy.

As they plodded along, Jenny could identify different formations in the rocks on either side of the path. Water, which had trickled into the concealed cave over the years, had dissolved some of the sculptured rock. It had left behind some strange, yet beautiful features.

At the beginning of the interesting trail, Jennifer had noticed what looked like ripples or waves in the flat rocks on the sides of the narrow passage. All of these figures reminded her of her mother's baked desserts. They looked somewhat like frosting which has gently flowed over the sides of a cake. As they hiked deeper into the bleak cave, Jenny felt a slight slope downward. The intriguing formations gradually changed into enormous stalagmites growing up from the cave floor. Stalactites hung precariously down from the dripping ceiling. Some of these two spellbinding shapes had grown together to form thick columns.

Once, when the speechless fairy flashed the lantern light on a vertical wall, Jenny could see a waterfall of stone. It startled her for a moment. She expected to hear water splashing, but the fake waterfall was not white. The stone fall was a brownish color as were all the natural formations that Jenny had seen that day. Sometimes Jennifer could glimpse a few bent helictites which were growing sideways out of overhanging rocks. In little recesses in the cave wall she saw sparkling, delicate, spiral crystals. These glistened as the light reflected off them.

A gigantic stone drapery hung a few dozen feet in front of the dirt path. It was near this that the mysterious fairy decided to stop the descent. Their feet stopped moving. All was silent in the dank cave except for the little scurrying sounds that troglobites make.

"Don't be frightened by those noises," the subdued woman told Jennifer. "There are rare beetles, spiders, and some types of salamanders living in this cave. They are all blind because of the absence of light." She added, "While we rest here, why don't you tell me about your travels to my island?"

Jennifer began by explaining to the attentive fairy that her mother was ill. She told her about floating in the sky inside a soap bubble to the birds' island. She recounted how kind and helpful the unusual birds, the whale pair and the artistic octopi had been.

"Since I've been gone, I have desperately wished that I had been kinder to my mother. I should have been trying to make her feel better by playing cards with her or reading to her. I was very selfish when I kept asking my parents to go places when I knew my mom didn't feel good. I thought I was too small to help. Now I know I can do a lot. I'll be different when I get back home."

When Jenny finished her complicated story it was evident that the antique lantern was not shining as brightly as it had been. Was it this lack of light which made the slim fairy's dress more brown than pink? Was it also the dim glow that seemed to change the enduring maiden's shiny black hair to a dull brown? And why were the secretive fairy's beautiful silk wings shriveled to a smaller dusty shape?

Jennifer was startled by a chilling draft that came from the depths of the cheerless cave. She heard water dribbling in front of her, but she could not see it. The reserved fairy scrutinized Jenny as she listened intently to the bubbling spring. The shuddering girl wrapped her arms tightly across her chest trying to warm herself.

"Have we come to the spring?" she asked the vigilant fairy anxiously. "I am beginning to feel cold and hungry. I would really like to find the spring and collect some of its fluid. Can you take me to the fountain, please?"

"I will take you there, but it will be difficult for you to leave," the fairy replied mysteriously.

Before Jennifer could ask why, the furtive woman turned and started to hobble on ahead. She was clenching the grimy lantern directly in front of her which made it awkward for Jenny to see the sunless path. The trembling girl was certain now though, the fairy's ugly dress was a dark brown and she had no wings at all. And why had her gliding stride been altered to a faltering step?

Because of the harsh blackness swallowing her, Jennifer needed both of her arms outstretched. She held one stiffly in front of her and one rigidly to the side for guidance. She stumbled clumsily every few feet as anyone does who is blindfolded and is not sure of her unknown surroundings.

"Please slow down," Jenny called out to the elusive fairy.

The puzzling woman did not answer. Jennifer could hardly see a faint light bouncing far into the gloom.

After about twenty minutes, Jennifer could again hear water rippling. She had not been able to catch the sound continuously because of all the turns the scant passage had taken. Now it was booming in this hushed environment and sounded as if it was next to her on her right side.

From the darkness, the baffled girl suddenly heard a hoarse voice. It was not the sweet voice of

the protective fairy who she had met that morning. This voice rattled and was definitely not pleasant. Jennifer was shivering already from the cold of the cave. After she heard the waiting fairy speak she had goose bumps running up her tensed spine.

"Here is your precious spring," the hissing voice said. "You may look as long as you like. In fact, you will remain here with me forever. I need someone to serve me."

Jenny could see a deformed shape lurking before her now. It was not the graceful figure that had willingly guided her. The wonderful fairy had been transformed into a gigantic black beetle. Her sheer wings were no longer visible. Her hideous body was covered with a hard exoskeleton that gave off a putrid odor.

As the grotesque insect waved its jointed legs in the air, it was apparent that the deformed beetle was blind. It did not really know exactly where the terrified girl stood.

Fifteen
Escape

Jennifer was stunned. She stared at the enormous insect that blocked her way in a menacing manner. Afraid to move forward, Jenny glanced to her right again. She strained her sore eyes to see the noisy fountain. She knew she must get to the solitary spring. She had to drain some of its distinctive liquid for her mother, but how? She had nothing to carry it in even if she could sneak past the scary beetle.

"What do you want me to do for you?" she asked the unsightly animal. "Remember that I am only a child. Some things are not possible for me."

"You need not worry," the gruesome insect replied. "I need food and you can collect it for me as easily as anyone. You have been very successful in your endeavors the past few days."

"What do you want me to bring you? I don't have anything to use for a basket and I can't see in the dark anyway," Jennifer answered wearily. She was hoping to convince the demanding brute that she was helpless. Then she might be able to leave the rotten cave.

"You may use the lantern for light to search for my food," suggested the monstrous beetle as it grinded its sharp jaws hungrily. "I eat dead salamanders which cover the floor of some of the cavern chambers. Sometimes I catch a stray bird when it flies close to the cave entrance."

Comprehending this unexpected news Jennifer hastily sat down. She felt very queasy. Maybe this ugly bug had captured Dusty. How would she ever know for sure? The apprehensive girl did not think she would be able to pick up dead animals to bring back to this hideous insect.

Jenny took a good, long look at the misshapen beetle. The crooked antennae were long and constantly waved as though the repulsive insect was nervous that Jenny might steal past it. The curved wing sheaths on its back were ink black. They masked what was left of the gorgeous transparent wings that had graced the fairy's back earlier. The beetle's snapping jaws were grinding even though it had no food in its wide mouth. Jenny reasoned that the offensive bully must smell so terrible because of the rancid diet it ate.

The commanding insect hissed, "I once found a large jar washed up on the beach. I dragged it down here by the fountain. I hoped that one day I might trap a human to serve me in the depths of my cave. You have fulfilled my wish. Now stop asking so many silly questions. Grab that jar and find me some food immediately. I can sense your presence with my antennae so don't try to escape. I will find you and make your life here miserable."

The impatient beetle finished this revolting speech by pointing with one of its warped legs to the foamy spring. It was only about twenty feet away.

"There is the jar. Now take it and begin your search," rattled the tyrant.

Jennifer slowly stood up. She sneaked a few steps to her left while watching the gross bug. She wanted to determine if the sightless beetle really could sense where she was. The sentry beetle's antennae waved madly and its dreadful head turned in the girl's direction.

Jenny sighed forlornly and then tiptoed to her right in the direction of the rare spring. Halfway to the fountain, she seized the lone lantern that was very dimly lit. The impulsive fairy must have placed it there before her complete transformation.

A large glass container about the size of a quart pickle jar sat on a flat rock near the splashing spring. Jennifer suddenly had an idea! She grasped the big jar with her free hand. Quietly she placed the brittle jar into the streaming water. While she filled the breakable jar with this precious fluid, she spoke loudly to the ghastly beetle.

"I have found the container you described. It is caught between some wedged rocks. I am trying to free it," she shouted. "I wish I had more light so I could see better."

"Just make do with what you have or I might decide you really are not useful to me," refused the monster. "There are many obscure places in this unknown cavern where I could take you to remain with no light, no food, and no water. You wouldn't like that, would you?"

While the threatening beetle growled these angry words, Jennifer had been scowling. She was looking for the narrow path that they had used to arrive at the babbling spring. Out of the corner of her eye she could barely see it behind her and to the left.

Immediately the courageous girl made a hurried decision that she knew she could not change once she put her developing plan into action. She hauled the cumbersome jar out of the slick spring. It was full and heavy now. She must hold it with both hands. Leaving the scratched lantern on the mushy ground she turned quickly to her left.

Jennifer heard the perplexed beetle asking nervously, "What are you doing?"

Without answering, she bolted. The only thing she wanted to do was run—run fast without stopping.

Jenny sprinted down the rocky path in the enveloping dark. She needed at least one hand free to feel the rock walls on either side. She halted for an instant to pour some of the precious fluid onto the slippery path. The hefty jar would be easier to hold if it was lighter. Now she could place her hand over the lip of the smooth jar. As she did this, she could hear close behind her the scuffling of the hunting beetle's legs stalking her.

The searching insect had a definite advantage since it could sense Jenny's presence with its sensitive antennae. Jenny had only the solid darkness all around her and she had to grope with her empty hand.

Soon after she dumped some of the contents of the jar on the musty dirt, she heard a sliding sound. Then she listened to angry mutterings. Jennifer knew that the mad beetle had slipped in the wet spot. She hoped that this would slow it down somewhat.

Right away though, she heard dragging feet and grumbling words coming after her closely again. Now Jennifer was huffing as she darted, but still trying to check her breathing and be quiet. She did not want to supply the possessive beetle with any more clues of her location.

The difficult trail turned here and there, leading Jenny on a seemingly endless trip. She thought how wondrous the sinister cavern had seemed before. Even if she had the beetle's lantern with her, she could not have paused to enjoy the rock formations now. They would only remind her of an inescapable cell. She squinted her eyes as she moved, hoping to see desired daylight around the next curve.

Finally, after what seemed to be hours, Jennifer could make out a tiny white pin spot of light directly in front of her. Just as she began to awkwardly race toward it, the persistent beetle's shufflings grew closer and closer. Instantly Jenny's feet were pulled out from under her. She landed face down on the hard path in the dimness.

Jennifer fingered warm blood on her scraped chin. She wiped it angrily away with one hand. Using her right hand as a lever she lifted herself up. The foul beetle was stepping on her right foot preventing her near escape.

Jenny sucked in a big breath and squeezed her eyes closed. She was certain that the loathsome insect was so angry with her that it would strike her.

Taunting her, it jeered, "Try to free yourself now."

In the next second she did not feel an expected blow. Jennifer heard a distinct rumbling sound like thunder. It seemed to come from the inner depths of the imprisoning cave. Then without warning, the trembling was overhead. Masses of dirt fell on Jenny and then larger and larger stones and rocks crashed down around her. She understood what was making the crumbling noise. Some of the old limestone from above had been loosened somehow. Maybe dripping water or the insane beetle's thumpings had caused the tremendous damage.

Before she could warn the dumbfounded insect, the unattached ceiling of the confined path began to tumble and fall on top of them. As the bulky rocks struck the captured beetle's body, it released its stand on Jennifer. Instinctively she darted in the direction of the light at the end of the unblocked passage.

Jenny did not cease running to look back at the trapped insect or the smashing rocks. She did not care if the horrifying beetle was trailing her or not. Her only thought was to get to daylight and safely away from the cave-in.

Within a few moments she had stumbled her way to the coveted entrance. It was not until then that she remembered that she had forgotten the elusive jar of spring water for her mother. Exhausted and disheartened, she collapsed outside the depressing cave. Gasping for breath, she plopped down in the dirt and propped herself up against a tree trunk.

Sixteen
Dreams of Home

Jennifer looked blankly at the vast ocean. What could she do? She did not know if the forgotten jar of precious fluid was broken. She could not retrace her steps into the collapsed cave to find it though. Now that she was free of the evil beetle, she was certain that she would never be able to make herself go back to the deadly cave-in to search for the abandoned jar. What if the disgusting insect was waiting for her?

How could she return home now? That was the most important issue in the world to her. She was little, but she had proven she could do good things. She would be able to help her mother, even if it meant just being there for her. But she had no means to travel. She had recklessly lost her bubble solution when she swam to the perilous island.

Was it only yesterday when she had pulled herself, soaked to the skin, onto the deserted beach? Now she was gazing at the evening sun as it set down into the endless sea. She felt so entirely helpless and lonely that her eyes began to fill with heartbroken tears.

While Jennifer stared pitifully at the bright pink-orange sun slowly immersing itself in the frothy ocean, her chaotic adventures of the past few days flashed through her mind. She thought fondly of Tiger and Dusty, her new friends. She contemplated the royal purple peacock, the charitable pigeons, and the tolerant owls that had befriended her. She remembered the protective whale and the cooperative flying fish that had helped her reach this wretched island. And then feeling a haunting shiver zip down her back, she recalled the fascinating pink fairy and the ridiculous savage that she became.

Jenny must have really been concentrating on her memory of the shimmering wings of the mutated fairy. She imagined she could even see a glistening shape on the sloping beach a few yards in front of her. What was the shining object revealed in the beige sand? Jennifer arose and crept toward the silver item. She gradually realized what it could be. Her floundering feet carried her faster to it. It was the shabby cover of her bubble bottle! It was still tightened around the shoddy container!

She raised the light bottle and shook it carefully. The hopeful girl heard sloshing. There was still some soap solution left. She would be able to return home! Jenny was cold and she was starving and she was thirsty, but she would not think of these problems now. She would blow a bubble and float away from this dreadful place right away.

Jenny nervously unscrewed the dented bottle cap. She withdrew the bubble wand from its container and dipped it in and out of the dwindling solution three times. She blew gently into the flimsy center of the soap film. Nothing happened. She puffed earnestly, but the clear membrane only popped. Once more she drew the rigid wand in and out of the diminishing solution and coaxed the film. Again nothing happened.

No giant bubble appeared to wrap itself securely around her. Jennifer yearned to hug her parents—her wonderfully gentle mother and devoted father. They must both be so worried about her. And here she was stranded on this forsaken island.

Jennifer shut her tearful eyes. She prayerfully dipped the bubble wand into the container again. When she pulled it out she shivered with cold. Her slippery hand shook and accidentally released its hold on the bubble bottle. It tumbled and spilled its irreplaceable contents all over the absorbent sand at her feet. Jenny was desperate now.

With a beseeching wish and a slow, even blow on the final film, a graceful shining orb gradually surrounded the tired body of the girl. She huffed until the delicate wall enclosed her on every side. Then with one gentle puff on the membrane above her head, the exceptional bubble lifted off the sparkling sand.

Rising upward over the tidal beach, Jennifer listened to the calm breeze blowing the drifting sphere.

Then she detected another comforting sound she recognized—wings flapping. Dusty was flying toward her quickly! He circled the inflated bubble twittering, "Jenny, where have you been? I've been looking all over the island for you."

"Dusty, how did you get to the island?" Jennifer questioned him excitedly.

The missing sparrow explained, "I had some trouble at first. When the bubble burst, one of my wings dipped slightly into the water. I couldn't fly high, but I fluttered above the ocean for a ways. Thank heavens I landed on a bobbing piece of faded driftwood. I perched on it until my damp wing dried as it floated around the island."

"Dusty, I was afraid you had unfortunately landed in the ocean." Jenny didn't tell him her real fear had been that the greedy beetle had captured him. "I've been inside a spooky cave," she said. "I am sorry that I was not able to bring any liquid out though. I guess I will not be able to help my mother after all. Can you come home with me?"

"I'm sorry, Jenny, but I have my own family on the birds' island. I need to go back. Good luck to you. I'll think of you often."

Jennifer understood and responded somberly, "Thank you for all your help. I'll never forget you, Dusty."

She solemnly waved good-bye to Dusty as he flew southward.

Higher and higher she floated as she had twice before. Jennifer did not look back. She could not bear to glimpse again the banana-shaped island where she had taken such positive hopes for her mother. She gazed down at the limitless ocean which was a deep navy blue color at this time of the evening. She regarded the wisps of pink-orange clouds above her. She was not happy, yet not sad. She was not afraid, and was not feeling brave. She was immensely relieved.

Somehow Jenny was confident that she would be home soon. She trusted that the glittering sphere would be blown in the correct direction. She allowed herself one last sleep, curled up inside her shielding globe. With her dainty chin resting on her knee, she fell asleep listening to the peaceful whispering of the air pushing the wobbling orb on its way.

Feeling considerable bumps like she had felt last summer when she rode her cousin's horse, Jennifer awoke drowsily and looked around the wafting bubble. It must have met some jumbled air currents as it floated down the coast. She could see her quiet city set near the sandy beach. She could barely even make out her welcoming back porch from the position in the sky at this time.

The protective bubble was drifting over the churning surf now, but it was dropping lower every second toward the wet sand. She wondered how long she had slept and how the eventful sphere had been directed toward her home. The magical bubble touched the solid beach and promptly burst.

Jenny glanced around her and was glad that it was evening. No one was there on the sunset beach to see her unusual arrival. Good, she did not know how she would explain about the bubble ride and her sudden appearance from the clouds. She was not certain herself how the enchanted bubble found its way home. She was sure that she could not tell others about her amazing adventure—not yet anyway.

Walking hurriedly, Jennifer made her way home. She only had to climb a few sand dunes and walk a block of sidewalk. There was her back porch—the same back porch where she had blown numerous bubbles a few days before. She noticed a child care magazine on the porch chair.

From the deserted backyard Jenny could hear mumbled voices inside her house. She was sure that she heard her father's calm voice. Jennifer was afraid for a moment that her mother had grown worse while she had been gone. Then she overheard her mother's silky tone. She hastened into the sunny kitchen and down the short hallway to her parents. As Jenny entered the living room, there was a stunned silence. Her parents were sitting together on the pale blue couch. Her mother rose first and ran to her with open arms crying, "Jenny, my doctor just called with such wonderful news! He has confirmed some recent tests he had done."

Before the astonished girl had a chance to speak, her grinning father had his arms around Jenny and her mother in one smothering hug. Giving her mother another long embrace, Jenny smiled like a painted circus clown.

Mrs. Waverly motioned for Jennifer to sit down beside her on the velvet sofa. "We have some terrific news for you, Jenny. I have not been feeling well the past few months as you know. I am much better now. I feel it is safe to tell you that I am going to have a baby in six months. Finally you will have a new sister or brother to love. We did not want you to know until now. We were afraid to disappoint you if I couldn't carry the baby. I'm not as young as I was when you were born. I will depend on you for help."

Jennifer could hardly believe her ears—a baby! She beamed with delight. Her parents cuddled next to her as they all put troublesome thoughts of the last months behind them and imagined their happy future.